Death's Daughter

and the Basket of Kittens

Martha Hull

Copyright © 2014 by Martha Hull

All rights reserved. No part of this book may be reproduced or transmtted in any form or by any means, electronic or mechanical, including photocopying, recording, or by any information storage and retrieval system, without permission in writing from the publisher, except in the case of brief quotations embodied in critical reviews and certain other noncommercial uses permitted by copyright law.

Published by:
Fluffpocalypse, LLC
Portland, Oregon

www.fluffpocalypse.com

www.marthahull.com

ISBN: 978-0-9858353-2-3

Printed in China

Thank you, Kickstarter.

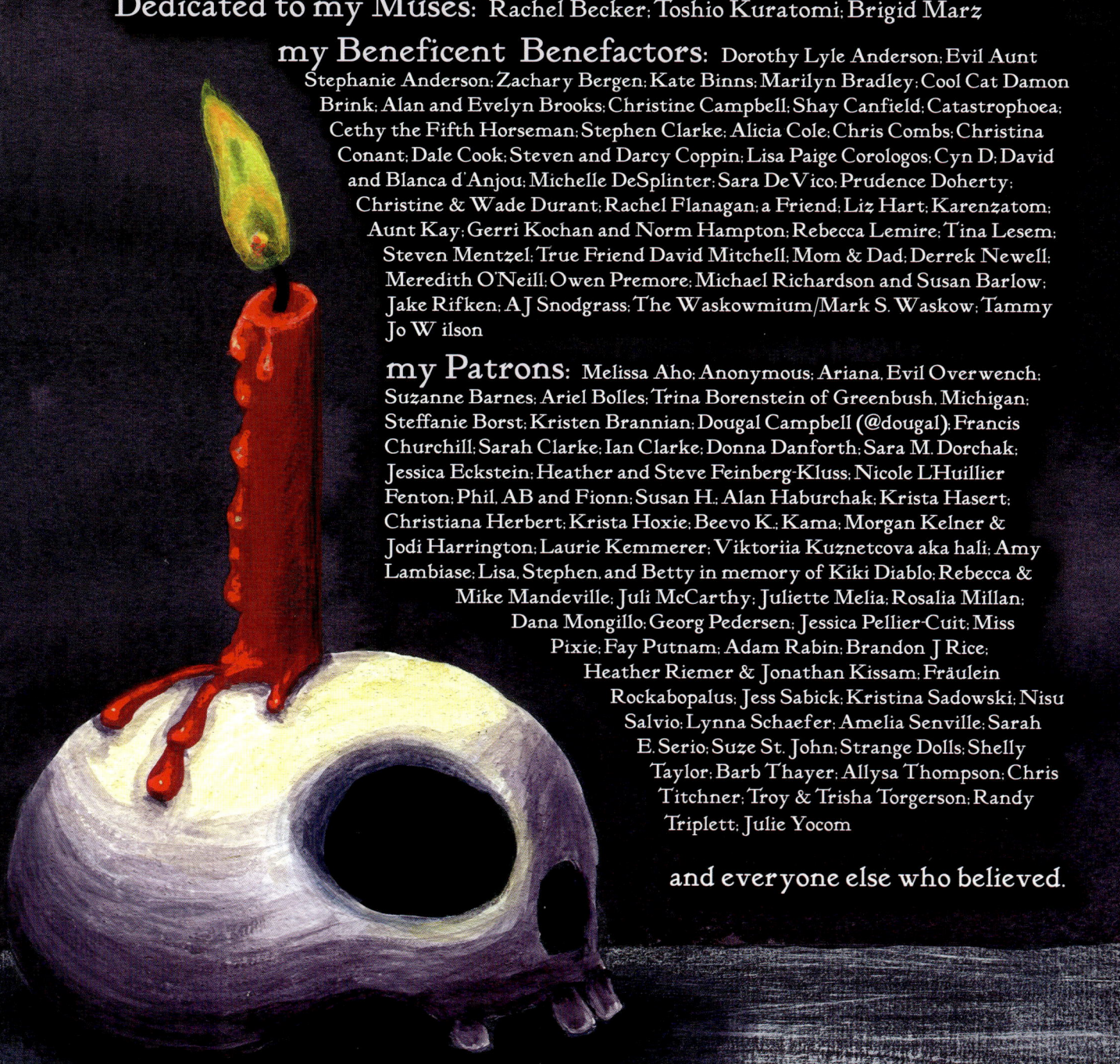

Dedicated to my Muses: Rachel Becker; Toshio Kuratomi; Brigid Marz

my Beneficent Benefactors: Dorothy Lyle Anderson; Evil Aunt Stephanie Anderson; Zachary Bergen; Kate Binns; Marilyn Bradley; Cool Cat Damon Brink; Alan and Evelyn Brooks; Christine Campbell; Shay Canfield; Catastrophoea; Cethy the Fifth Horseman; Stephen Clarke; Alicia Cole; Chris Combs; Christina Conant; Dale Cook; Steven and Darcy Coppin; Lisa Paige Corologos; Cyn D; David and Blanca d'Anjou; Michelle DeSplinter; Sara DeVico; Prudence Doherty; Christine & Wade Durant; Rachel Flanagan; a Friend; Liz Hart; Karenzatom; Aunt Kay; Gerri Kochan and Norm Hampton; Rebecca Lemire; Tina Lesem; Steven Mentzel; True Friend David Mitchell; Mom & Dad; Derek Newell; Meredith O'Neill; Owen Premore; Michael Richardson and Susan Barlow; Jake Rifken; AJ Snodgrass; The Waskowmium/Mark S. Waskow; Tammy Jo Wilson

my Patrons: Melissa Aho; Anonymous; Ariana, Evil Overwench; Suzanne Barnes; Ariel Bolles; Trina Borenstein of Greenbush, Michigan; Steffanie Borst; Kristen Brannian; Dougal Campbell (@dougal); Francis Churchill; Sarah Clarke; Ian Clarke; Donna Danforth; Sara M. Dorchak; Jessica Eckstein; Heather and Steve Feinberg-Kluss; Nicole L'Huillier Fenton; Phil, AB and Fionn; Susan H.; Alan Haburchak; Krista Hasert; Christiana Herbert; Krista Hoxie; Beevo K.; Kama; Morgan Kelner & Jodi Harrington; Laurie Kemmerer; Viktoriia Kuznetcova aka hali; Amy Lambiase; Lisa, Stephen, and Betty in memory of Kiki Diablo; Rebecca & Mike Mandeville; Juli McCarthy; Juliette Melia; Rosalia Millan; Dana Mongillo; Georg Pedersen; Jessica Pellier-Cuit; Miss Pixie; Fay Putnam; Adam Rabin; Brandon J Rice; Heather Riemer & Jonathan Kissam; Fräulein Rockabopalus; Jess Sabick; Kristina Sadowski; Nisu Salvio; Lynna Schaefer; Amelia Senville; Sarah E. Serio; Suze St. John; Strange Dolls; Shelly Taylor; Barb Thayer; Allysa Thompson; Chris Titchner; Troy & Trisha Torgerson; Randy Triplett; Julie Yocom

and everyone else who believed.

Belladonna's mother died the night she was born.

It was not a coincidence.

Belladonna had inherited her father's powers.

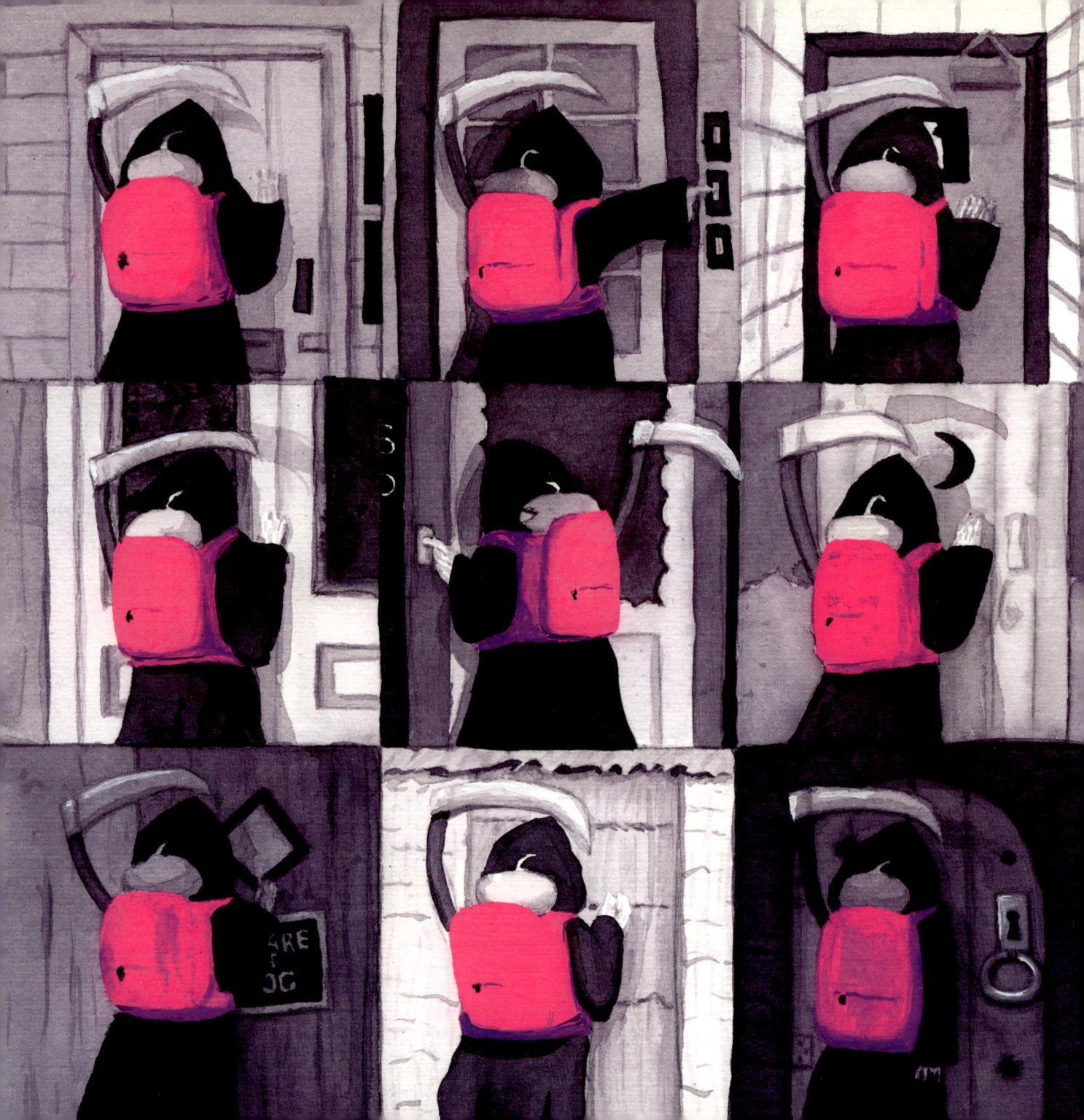

Often, she was lonely.

One day, a friend came along!

after day.

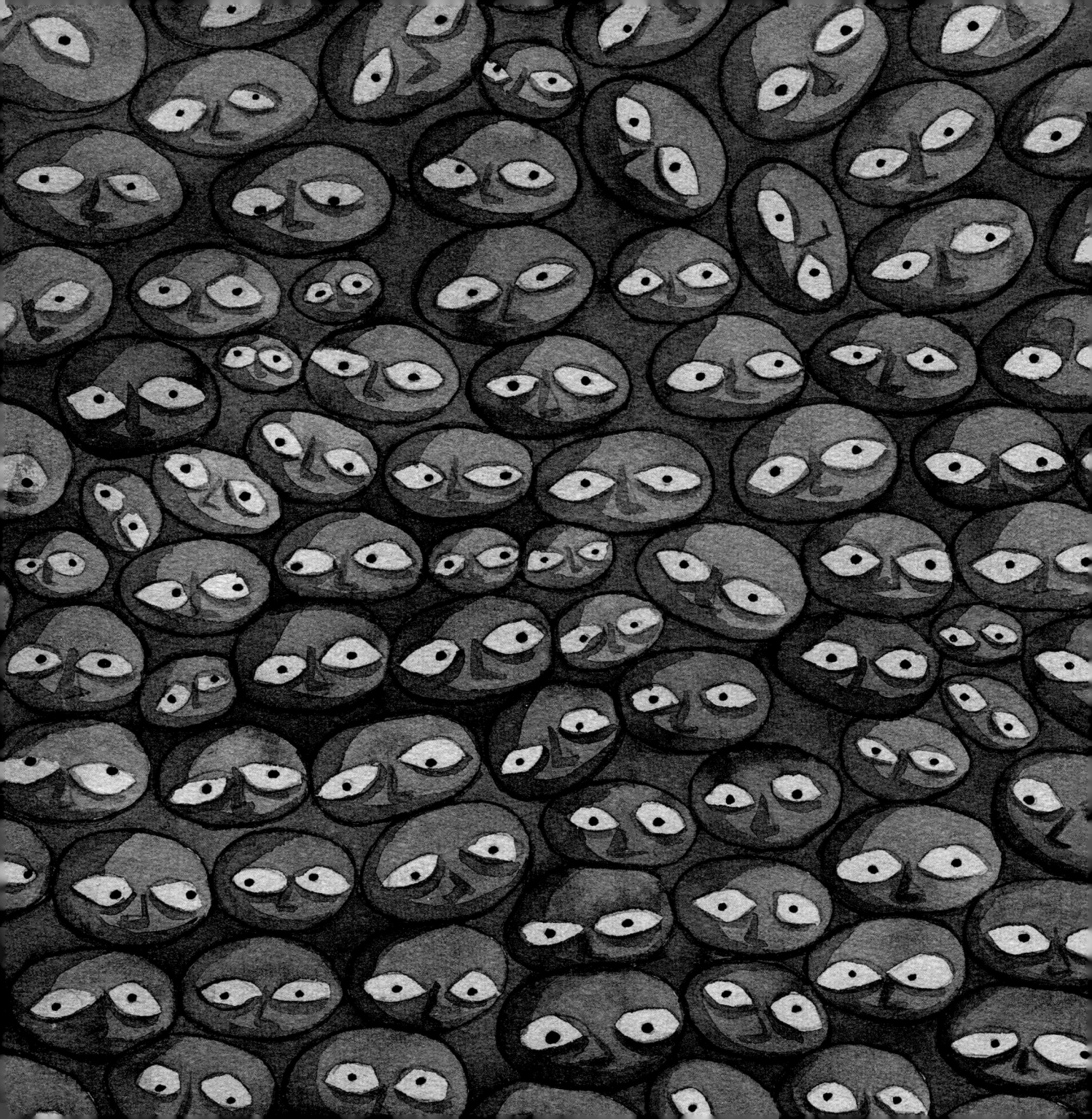

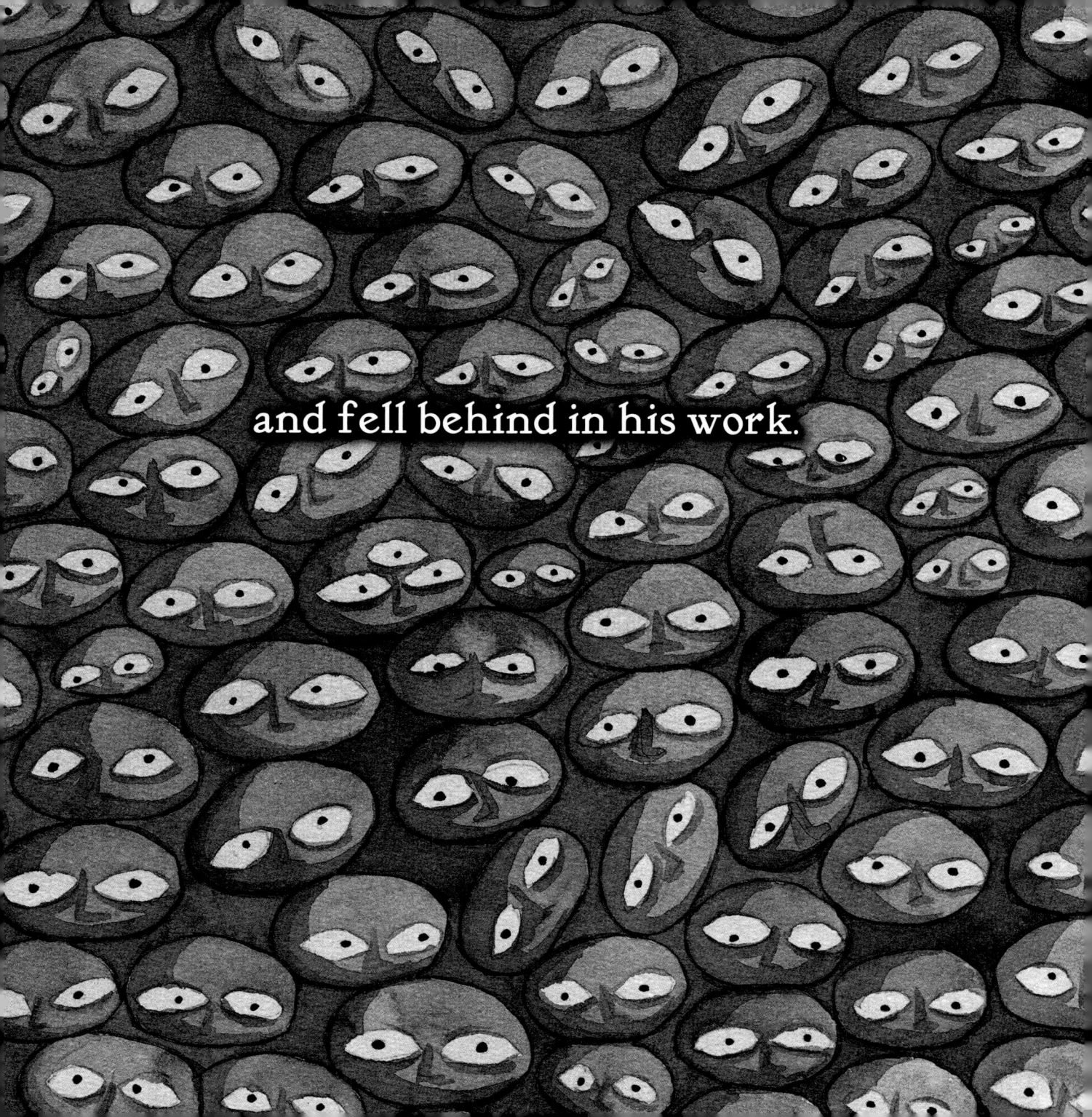

She named them Strife, Pestilence, Famine,

With the kittens to absorb her powers, Belladonna decided to visit her friend.

Some people had taken away all the grass and trees.

Belladonna went home.

A new day dawned.

Death ventured forth.

He took his daughter everywhere.